Drive Thru

THE BEGINNING OF
BREAD

by Harriet Brundle

The Sandwich Shack

BEARPORT
PUBLISHING

Minneapolis, Minnesota

Credits

All images are courtesy of Shutterstock.com, unless otherwise specified.
With thanks to Getty Images, Thinkstock Photo, and iStockphoto.

Front Cover - GoodVector, Five Stars, Fast Illustration, Tsekhmister, 2&3 - Natykach Nataliia, 4&5 - Incomible, bunnavit pangsuk, 6&7 - Timmary, Gamzova Olga, Nitr, wideonet, 8&9 - Wanwisspaul, Africa Studio, muchomoros, Matrela, Fascinadora, 10&11 - WAYHOME studio, sweet marshmallow, 12&13 - Amanuta Silvicora, ZigZag Mountain Art, ao nori, vikpoint, MagicBones, AnkitPatel004, 14&15 - Moving Moment, AROONA, jehsomwang, 16&17 - jehsomwang, Supitcha McAdam, Caron Badkin, monicaodo, 18&19 - Richard M Lee, TP71, janosmarton, Brent Hofacker, Marie C Fields, Bartosz Luczak, f o g a a s, 20&21 - Asya Nurullina, hadasit, Vladislav Noseek, fumi901, N K, 22&23 - Reamolko, GB_Art.

Library of Congress Cataloging-in-Publication Data

Names: Brundle, Harriet, author.
Title: The beginning of bread / Harriet Brundle.
Description: Fusion books. | Minneapolis, MN : Bearport Publishing Company, [2022] | Series: Drive thru | Includes bibliographical references and index.
Identifiers: LCCN 2021011419 | ISBN 9781647479473 (library binding) | ISBN 9781647479558 (paperback) | ISBN 9781647479633 (ebook)
Subjects: LCSH: Bread--Juvenile literature.
Classification: LCC TX769 .B8395 2022 | DDC 641.81/5--dc23
LC record available at https://lccn.loc.gov/2021011419

© 2022 Booklife Publishing
This edition is published by arrangement with Booklife Publishing.

North American adaptations © 2022 Bearport Publishing Company. All rights reserved. No part of this publication may be reproduced in whole or in part, stored in any retrieval system, or transmitted in any form or by any means, electronic, mechanical, photocopying, recording, or otherwise, without written permission from the publisher.

For more information, write to Bearport Publishing, 5357 Penn Avenue South, Minneapolis, MN 55419. Printed in the United States of America.

CONTENTS

Hop in the Sandwich Shack . . . 4
The Beginning of Bread 6
Start with the Dough. 8
Kneading and Resting 10
Get Your Bake On 12
Different Flavors. 14
More Ingredients 16
Making Shapes. 18
A World of Bread. 20
Bread Time! 22
Glossary 24
Index 24

HOP IN THE SANDWICH SHACK

Hi! My name is Hala, and this is my food truck, the Sandwich Shack! I use the best bread to make tasty sandwiches. Which one would you like to try?

* MENU *
Egg salad
Bánh mì
Grilled cheese
Katsu sando

Oh no! I'm out of bread! I need to get some more. Hop in the Sandwich Shack and join me!

The Sandwich Shack

THE BEGINNING OF BREAD

There are many different kinds of breads. Let's look at some of the breads I use on my truck.

Humans have made bread for around 14,000 years.

WHITE BREAD

PITA BREAD

White bread is soft, and baguettes are crusty. Pita bread is flat.

BAGUETTES

7

START WITH THE DOUGH

Bread can be made in lots of different ways. But most breads have the same basic **ingredients**. These are flour, water, **yeast**, and salt.

FLOUR

SALT

YEAST

WATER

To start, all the ingredients are mixed together to make **dough.**
1kg.
800
200
600
400

KNEADING AND RESTING

Then, the dough is **kneaded**. After kneading, the dough is left to rest. While it rests, the dough will **rise**.

Kneading can be done by hand or using a machine.

Bread dough rises because of yeast. The yeast makes tiny air bubbles in the dough.

Now, it's time to bake!

GET YOUR BAKE ON

Many kinds of bread are baked in an oven. But there are different ways to cook bread dough.

Bagels are boiled in water before being baked in an oven.

Injera

Tandoor oven

Naan can be cooked on the walls of a tandoor oven.

Injera is a bread that is cooked on a large, flat pan.

The Sandwich Shack

DIFFERENT FLAVORS

Other ingredients can be added to breads to give them different flavors. Some people add nuts, fruits, or cheeses.

A seeded loaf has seeds. They add flavor and crunch to the bread.

Poppy seeds

Pumpkin seeds

Sesame seeds

MORE INGREDIENTS

Whole wheat bread is made with whole wheat flour. The flour is brown. It gives the bread a darker color than white bread.

Some breads have herbs added for flavor.

Herbs

What is your favorite kind of bread?

The Sandwich Shack

17

MAKING SHAPES

Bread comes in different shapes, too. People form dough into a shape. They might twist it or roll it. The bread keeps this shape after it is baked.

KNOT

RING

BRAID

ROLL

TWIST

BAGUETTE

People can also cut a picture into the top of the dough. The picture will stay there when the bread is done baking!

A WORLD OF BREAD

Bread is eaten all over the world. Many people use bread to make sandwiches.

Baguettes are used to make bánh mì. This sandwich comes from Vietnam.

Pita bread is used to make sabich. This sandwich comes from Israel.

Katsu sandos come from Japan. They are made using white bread with the crusts cut off.

White bread is often used to make grilled cheese sandwiches.

Egg salad sandwiches can use white, wheat, or seeded bread.

BREAD TIME!

Hooray! We've made it back with lots of bread to make yummy sandwiches. Which one would you like to try?

The Sandwich

* MENU *
Egg salad
Bánh mì
Grilled cheese
Katsu sando

GLOSSARY

dough a sticky, thick mixture of flour, water, and other ingredients that is used to make bread

ingredients different things that are used to make food

kneaded pressed, folded, and stretched

rise to move upward

yeast an ingredient used in baking that helps things rise

INDEX

baking 11–12, 18–19
dough 8–12, 18–19
Israel 20
Japan 21
kneading 10
sandwiches 4–5, 20–22
tandoor oven 13
Vietnam 20
yeast 8, 11